Ebb and Flo

and [illegible] Gulls

Jane Simmons

ORCHARD BOOKS

To Celia

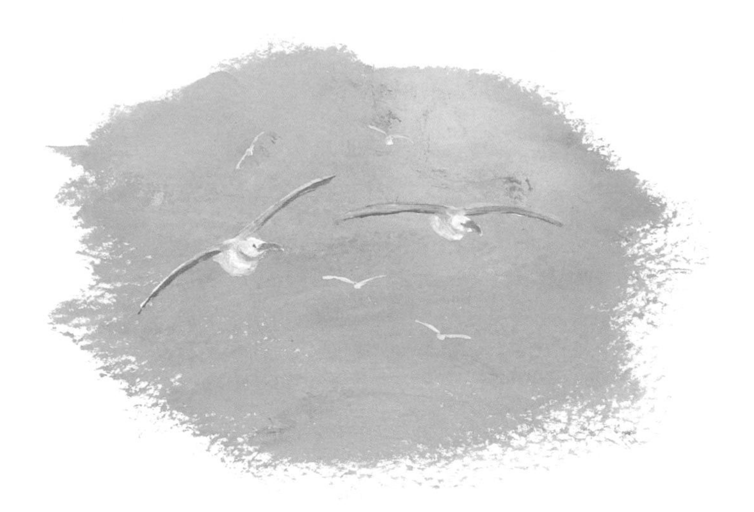

ORCHARD BOOKS
96 Leonard Street, London EC2A 4XD
Orchard Books Australia
32/45-51 Huntley Street, Alexandria, NSW 2015
ISBN 1 84362 841 4
First published in Great Britain in 1999
First paperback edition published in 2000
This edition published in 2005

A CIP catalogue record for this book is available from the British Library.
1 3 5 7 9 10 8 6 4 2
Printed in Singapore

It was a lovely day.
Ebb listened to the seagulls laughing.
Everything was wonderful.

Ebb closed her eyes and sniffed the sea air.
"Beep! Beep!" said Bird.
The seagulls laughed.

Ebb snoozed on the warm sand.

. . .but the seagulls came.
"Woof! Woof!" barked Ebb.
The seagulls just laughed at her.

"Ebb!" said Flo. "You've eaten
all the sandwiches!"
"Beep! Beep!" said Bird.
The seagulls laughed.

"You've eaten loads!" said Flo. "Oh, Ebb!"
"Oh! Ebb!" said Mum.
"Beep! Beep!" said Bird.
The seagulls laughed and Ebb sulked.

Ebb sulked in her favourite spot.
It was so unfair.

It began to rain and Mum and Flo
cleared the food away.
The seagulls swooped.
Waves lapped on the boat.
Ebb sulked.

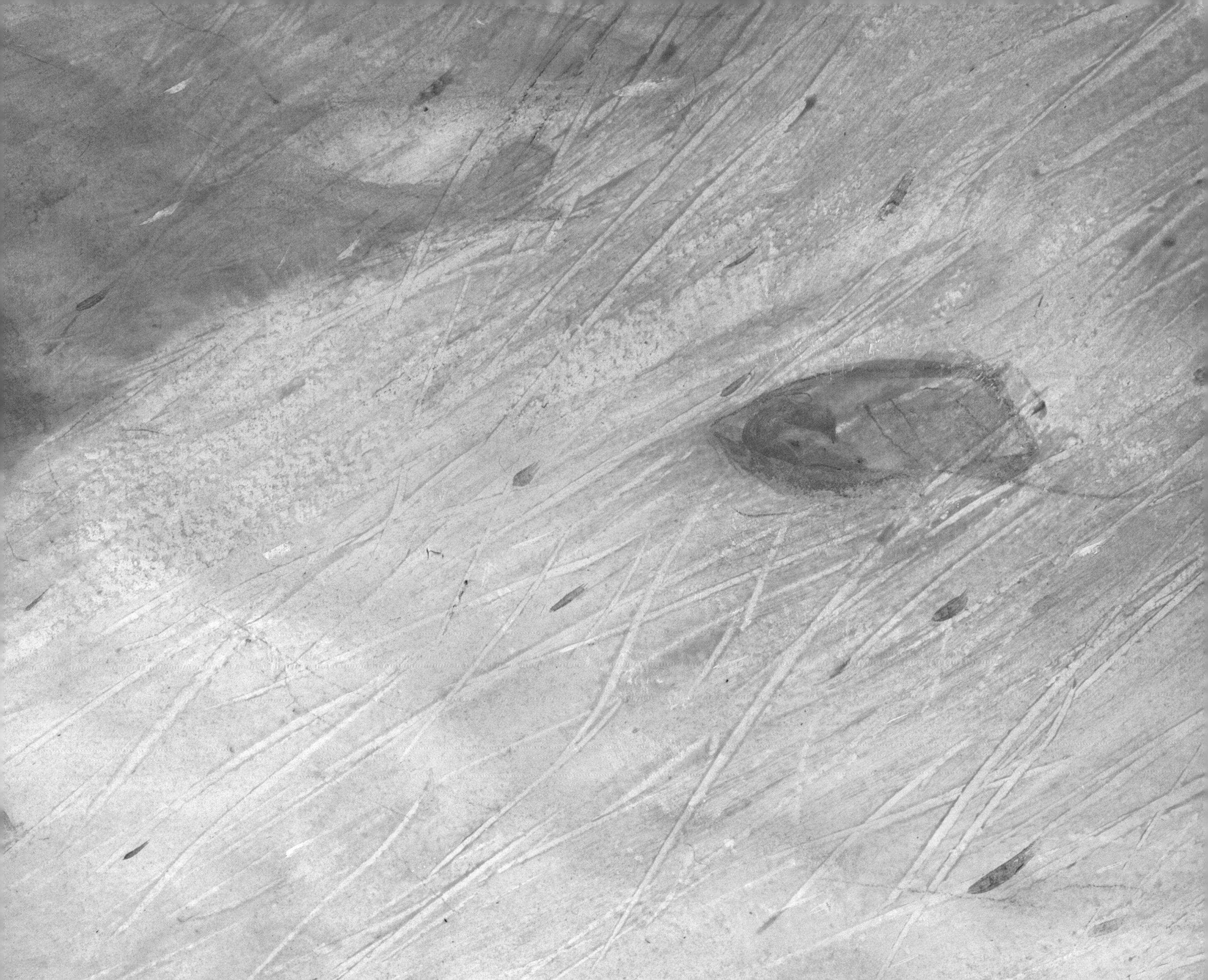

"It's the seagulls! *They're* taking the food!" cried Flo.
"Shoo!" shouted Mum.
"Beep! Beep!" said Bird.
The seagulls laughed.
Ebb sulked.

When she looked up, she was all alone.
The little boat was drifting out to sea.
"Woof! Woof!" said Ebb, but nobody came.

The little boat started to spin.
“Woof! Woof!” said Ebb.
It went around
and around, faster and. . .

faster and FASTER. . .
"Woof! Woof! Woof!"
barked Ebb.

CRASH!

"Where are you, Ebb?" shouted Flo.

Ebb looked up and there were Bird and Flo.
“Beep! Beep!”
“Oh, Ebb!” said Flo. “I’m sorry I blamed you.”

“I do love you so much,” she said,
and the seagulls laughed overhead.